Gay Erotic Romance

Gideon Elliot

A Second Chance

WARNING

This book contains sexually explicit scenes and adult language. It may be considered offensive to some readers. This book is for sale to adults ONLY.

Please store your files wisely where they cannot be accessed by underage readers.

* * * * * * * * * * * * * * * * * * *

WANT FREE COPIES OF MY BOOKS?
Just visit my blog and download free copies of my books:
http://gideon-elliot.awesomeauthors.org/gideon-elliot/

About the Publisher

4Fun Publishing, a member of **BLVNP Incorporated**, 340 S. Lemon #6200, Walnut CA 91789, info@blvnp.com / legal@blvnp.com
NOTE: Due to the highly emotional reaction of some people to works of erotic fiction, any email sent to the above address that contains foul language or religious references is automatically deleted by our anti-spam software and will not be seen. All other communications are welcome.

DISCLAIMER

A Second Chance
Gay Erotic Romance

By: Gideon Elliot

ISBN: 978-1-62761-377-4

Chapter 1

The stars fired the heavens with magnesium jets of desire. They burned in his eyes as he walked by the river. Never had he suffered such grievous despair as now he was feeling. He was flaming with desire and aching with the fear of feeling it.

The trucks were rolling under the West Side Highway and the moon looked like it would fall out of the sky, but it continued there nevertheless and it turned into a pallid stream of light, a band stretching across the black surface of the Hudson.

There was nothing to do but to go home and to go to sleep, hoping that the band of light might transform itself, in sleep, through sleep, into the multi-foliate shape of a dream -- such a dream as makes sleep more appealing than waking. But a dream can bear pain as well as pleasure, recapitulate torments undergone as well as realize wishes.

He woke confused. He had been a slave in a red Moroccan palace and wore only a cloth of gold skirted round his hips. He stood high like an Egyptian with his nipples stiff and commanding.

First thing he had to do was to try to remember what he had done last night.

Everything had been going smoothly in the days, the weeks, and the months before. He thought he had it beat this time. Miriam had been tender. She was no longer talking about leaving him and taking the children with her as she had that night two years ago when she'd called him a rotten bastard and cursed him for continuing his gay cruising even after the birth of the twins.

He had felt guilty enough to listen to her shouting without trying to defend himself. He did not want to go to Dr. Nostrand, but he did. For the sake of his marriage, he did. He pressed his lips together and vowed to give it his best shot. He'd been trying to beat this thing since he was twelve!

Nostrand took him by the upper arm and guided him into his office.

"Please," he said, pointing to a leather chair.

"I feel pain."

"You feel pain."

"I want something I'm not allowed to want. I feel something I must not feel."

"So it feels like pain when you have to stop yourself from feeling what you feel?"

"It feels like pain, yes."

"Then the solution is simple. You must feel what you want to feel and feel also that you are afraid to feel it. Yah. Expose all the feelings. Right now they are powerful because they are in hiding, waiting in ambush, using the darkness you are providing. They can jump out at you at any moment and overpower you because you can't see them."

"Yeah."

"So if you give them darkness, they can only get stronger and bide their time. No. You must acknowledge those feelings, bring them into the open. In the light you can see them. And then you can discard them."

So Andrew felt what he knew he felt. But now he felt it like it was something that existed, yes, but was not necessarily his. He could just pass it by.

Andrew thought it had worked. Miriam did, too. She had let down her guard. So had he.

So it was strange that suddenly -- (suddenly?) -- he was overwhelmed, as if he'd been hypnotized and given a post-hypnotic suggestion, by desire he did not want to have.

It was a hot August night. Miriam had flown with the children to her parents in Sussex for a fortnight, and he was busy at the office every day.

He got home Friday after seven, having spent a very long day doing research and writing briefs in the Spenser trial, which was on the docket before Judge Hermandiez for the second week of September.

"You're wasting your time, darling," O'Brien said, leaning against the window and watching the sunset illuminate the glass panels of a skyscraper neighboring the one which housed their offices.

"Huh?" Andrew said

"You're wasting your time. You'll never win this one."

"Whose side are you on?" Andrew said with indignation.

"Everyone knows Hermandiez is a ball buster."

"Maybe," Andrew said. "But, then again, maybe I got tough balls."

"Oh, butch!" O'Brien cried. "But, really, honey, you're a pussy."

Exhausted, hungry, unable to shake off O'Brien's smarmy insinuation, when he got home -- or was it just the heat? His mind was grinding on nothing, like the wheels of a car spinning in sand. Eating or resting, both were impossible.

He showered, shaved, toweled himself dry. He was pleased, turned on at how good he looked in the mirror. What a fool he'd been in his twenties when he was still caught up in a superficial gay boy sensibility and thought that thirty-seven was old.

He hadn't gone to The Web since, since he had tried to turn...to re-establish things with Miriam. But tonight, even as he drifted over there without being deliberate about it, once he was inside, he realized that a part of him had known all day long that that was where he was going to wind up.

* * *

He went home with a guy named Max Harrison who lived in a high-rise off Ninth Avenue on Twenty-third Street.

Harrison was a few years younger than Andrew, slightly taller than him, and well built, nicely muscled. His body was firm and hard.

"I'll give you a massage," Harrison said, sensing the tension that prevented Andrew from responding to him. "Lie down."

Andy stripped down to his black boxer briefs, smiled, and then took them off. He lay face down on a narrow bed in a long, narrow room painted maroon, lit only by candles.

Harrison warmed scented oil, lily of the valley, rubbing his palms together. He began with Andy's lower back, spreading out, slowly, gentle circles, warming his back with kneading fingers, playing the cords of his neck as if he were fingering a recorder. And like a recorder, Andrew began to sing in long high moans the tune being played upon him, the song of desire and surrender.

But before desire could peak or surrender drive him into wild submission, he spilled himself in a slow and senseless ooze.

"I can't stay," he said jumping up suddenly.

"It's okay," Harrison said, hoping to calm him. "Would you like some coffee before you go."

With shaking fingers he could hardly button his shirt or tie his shoes. He fled from the place into the street in panic.

* * *

It would have been the end of it, and everything would have been fine, except for one thing which made the situation incomplete and therefore unfinished and therefore a dangerously, damagingly lingering one. He could not stop thinking about Harrison. Or, at least, his body could not stop. And whenever his body thought about Harrison he became furiously sexually aroused.

When he went up to Harrison at The Web the next night when he was standing at the bar, Harrison snubbed him. It made sense. What else could he do? Andrew had walked out on him last night, left him high and dry. He was not a shrink or an eleemosynary institution for confused faggots. And he did not need serial blue balls. So he turned his back. It made sense.

But Andrew said, "I'm really sorry about last night, and I want to try it again."

"What the hell do you think I am?" Harrison turned from the torso and said.

"I know," Andy said. "I freaked out."

"What's it to me?" Harrison said. "I don't force people to be with me, but once they do choose to be, I expect they want to, that they know what they are doing."

"I'm really sorry," Andy said, "but I can't get you out of my mind."

"What do you want from me?" Harrison said, amusement and disdain expressing themselves in his voice and on his face. "Do you even know?"

"I'm not sure I do," Andy said, "but I know I can't get you out of my mind."

"Tell you what," Max said. "I'll give you a second try, but there have to be some stipulations."

"Stipulations?" Andrew said.

"Stipulations," Max repeated. "You know what that means?"

"I ought to," Andy said. "I'm a lawyer."

"So much the better," Max said. "Stipulations."

"Complete obedience, complete passivity, unconditional surrender."

He sounded like the very devil extending his most alluring possibilities.

And Andrew said he'd sign the contract. He meant it metaphorically, but the words felt eerie.

"Go home, now," Max said.

"What?" Andrew said not expecting that.

"Go home, now," Max repeated.

"But I thought..."

"There's no need for you to think," Max said, gently, consolingly, as if speaking to a confused child.

* * *

"But nothing happened," Andrew said hoping that would be enough. It was almost true, too.

It was not enough.

Miriam crushed her cigarette out in the seashell ashtray on her desk and exhaled a cloud of pungent smoke at the same time.

"What happened happened inside you," she said. "Whatever actually transpired is not important. What's important is..."

"My god," Andrew shouted. "You want to control every electrical impulse that tingles through me."

"I thought we had come to the point where you were able to acknowledge responsibility for your own behavior."

He took a deep breath and he felt the isolation in his heart that he had been damned with from birth. And every time it had been succoured, it was only temporary. But isolation was solid ground. Everybody else was a phantom you had to watch out for.

He moped around the house when he was not at work.

But at work, he felt himself in another world, free in the solitary of his active mind, formulating doctrines and making sense of human action through the mediating grill of the law, which, it seemed to him, was the only thing able to make experience sensible.

"I don't know what to do with you," she said.

He shuddered inside and held the ears of his soul to keep his tranquility undisturbed, but listened with the ears of his mind to try and figure out how he could improve and prove himself more satisfactory to her.

But sometimes he got tired of that and saw himself made up and costumed, serving in a candlelit chamber a beautiful boy who adored him, to whom he had surrendered his very soul.

* * *

He had in a stupid moment, given one of his e-mail addresses to Harrison.

"I will expect you this Friday at 9:30 at the bar at The Web."

That's all it said.

Andrew was inclined to ignore it but was drawn to linger over the message and read it again and again.

* * *

Miriam was irritable Friday morning as she was packing her small bag for a week in New Orleans where she was going for The National Book Association's annual convention. There were three titles, important books by important figures, a political memoir, a historical romance, and a critique of the policies of the present American government that she had particular interest in. She had shepherded them through printing and wanted to supervise how they were marketed, too.

She ought to have been excited. But she was uneasy. She reviewed the possible causes: anxiety about flying, fear that her books would not be well received, the same misgivings she always had as a mother leaving the children for any length of time. Sure, all those were possibilities. But, no, it was Andrew. Something was unsettled. She could not put her finger on it. But there was something disquieting in the air between them.

"Oh, well," she sighed and cleared her mind.

She was cheerful at parting when she got into the taxi for the airport, regretting that she had been irritable.

"Don't be too lonely without me. Don't let the kids run you ragged. Don't wear yourself out at work."

"Any do's?"

"Do think of me when..." She blushed. "You know when."

"And don't you exhaust yourself either," Andrew said. "The books are wonderful, and I know you'll be able to place them."

He left her and picked the kids up from school and took them to the health food restaurant for dinner and read the next chapter of *Silas Marner* to them before bed.

Once they were asleep, he mixed vodka and grapefruit juice over ice and sipped slowly as he looked over his e-mails.

As if in a trance, he changed his clothes to an old, torn pair of jeans and motorcycle boots.

He stood in front of the mirror trying to decide whether to put on a white sleeveless athletic shirt or a black one. He played idly with his nipples which seemed to stretch with undefined desire and stiffen.

He chose a square-topped white tight-fitting top.

"Margie," he said, speaking into his cell-phone. "It's Andrew. Is it ok if I go out for awhile and you keep an eye and ear open for the kids?"

Margie was a downstairs neighbor. She had a key to the apartment and often looked after the kids when Andrew or Miriam wanted to go out.

"Sure," she said. "Mind if I go through your DVD collection."

"Not at all, Marge."

"Or if I fall asleep on your couch?"

"Of course not. Thanks so much! There's some cold Raki in the fridge, too."

* * *

It was chilly enough that he could wear his leather jacket but still not so chilly that you couldn't leave it unzipped.

He was a little self-conscious about his nipples, but he also liked it, the way they pressed against the tight fabric. He breathed deeply and stretched his pecs upward.

The smell of beer hit him as he pushed his way into The Web and over to the bar.

"Hello," Andrew said to Max.

"I want a vodka martini," was all Harrison said, but it was clear he expected Andrew to bring it to him.

"Yes sir." Andrew had intended it to sound cheeky. But it didn't. It didn't sound anything out of the ordinary.

Andrew came back with the martini for Max and had gotten one for himself, too.

Harrison laughed and waved a finger.

"No, no," he said. "That is not done. You don't get anything for yourself without getting my permission first."

Andrew pulled a disbelieving face and Harrison said in a low voice, smiling, as if he were speaking of love, speaking slowly, "If you're going to be my bitch, you're going to follow my rules. Put your drink down next to mine. You drink if and when I say you do."

By the time he left the bar, Andrew, with Harrison's permission had drunk enough martinis to make him stagger giddily.

"You really ought to not drink so much if you can't hold it," Max laughed pressing him tightly to himself, steadying him as they walked.

"But you said I could," Andrew teased back, looking into his eyes and stumbling because he could not see what he was doing.

"And do you do everything I say?" Harrison asked with an amused grin.

"I do," Andrew said. "I absolutely do."

"How do you account for that?" Harrison taunted him.

"Because...just because."

Chapter 2

It really did not need to be New Orleans. Inside, it hardly was. There were identical hotel rooms painted Dresden green. There were long corridors gussied up to look like a street lined with bistros. There were Grand Ballrooms, one painted a butter color; the other, avocado. There were silvered hot plates at long buffets. But outside, it was New Orleans. She left the hotel and walked around the quarter glad that it had been preserved.

"Well, I'll be."

It was Richard Spurge from Harper's new religious division.

"You still mad at me?" he said falling in step beside her.

"I wasn't mad at you," she said. "I was just bothered that you were doing that. I remember you from college, Richard. Bertrand Russell: *Why I Am Not A Christian*. Thick paperback. Remember? It goes against everything you once...I mean..."

She stopped, blushed, stumbled verbally but picked herself up.

"You're, I don't know. You could do better. You... Books are for opening people's minds, not closing them. So I got angry because you know that, or you once did. And now, you're acting like you don't know it anymore."

"You know, you're beautiful," he said.

"When I get angry?"

"No, when you get thoughtful and analytic."

She looked at him suspiciously.

"No, I mean it. I know what you're saying. But you don't understand. Sometimes you have to go where they put you, or you don't get to go anywhere and you won't even have a home to stay in if all you want to do is just stay home."

She shook her head. Darkness and concern showed themselves in the furrows she made in her brow.

"Do you want an anti-depressant?"

"What?"

"Do you want an anti-depressant?" she repeated. "It's quite mild. I couldn't go on sometimes without. Might do you good."

* * *

"With you concord is an event within discord," she said carrying a bag of groceries into the house up the flagstone path.

Andrew preceded her by a few steps carrying the heavier bag and fumbling for his keys.

"I want a relationship," she said, "where, when discord happens -- I know it has to -- discord is an event inside concord, surrounded by it."

"What are you saying?" he said, pushing open the back door into the kitchen,

"I'm not going to go on like this." she said, standing by the table upon which she had just set down her bag.

"What do you want to happen?" He hesitated to ask. He was ashamed of the passivity he felt himself locked into.

"I want you to leave."

He looked impassively into the void.

"What about the kids?" It was not insistent. It was a murmur.

"When have you ever cared about them?" she said reproachfully. She still stood by the table, not moving. He wished she would so he could move. It was as if he could not move unless she released him.

"And now you're using them to make yourself look pitiable," she continued.

She spat the last words. There was nothing you could say. But everything was off. She was right. What could he argue? Discord was at the center of their marriage.

"Oh, don't look like that," she said. "I won't buy it. I know you're just waiting to go. But you're too guilty to say what you want. People like you are dangerous."

* * *

"You're somewhere," Max said, rubbing Andrew's shoulders.

"Yeah, I sure am."

"Tell me. What's going on? Where are you?"

"I'm on Thirty-Second Street."

"I don't understand."

"I'm living in a hotel on Thirty-Second Street."

"Not at home?"

"I have no home."

Silence.

"Miriam kicked me out."

"What will you do?"

"I don't know. The only thing that keeps me going is work."

"Thanks," Harrison said, teasingly.

"This – you and me – it doesn't feel real, Max. I'm sorry. I don't know. It's like kids playing follow the leader."

"You mean that?"

"Half and half. I mean it feels good but..."

"But now there's nothing keeping you from making it real."

"You mean?"

"What do you mean?"

"Are you talking about us living together?"

"Do you want to?"

"Me moving in here?"

"There's a spare room, although I think we should share the bedroom."

"But I'm supposed to feel bad."

"And you don't?"

"May I be honest?"

Max nodded assent.

"The thought of living with you excites me very much, of being that close to you. It's a feeling I've only experienced fleetingly. I never thought it was really meant for me."

"That means you don't have to go home. You can sleep here tonight."

"I'm free."

"You're home."

* * *

Richard Spurge took Miriam to a small restaurant on Mercer Street where they ate octopus and stuffed red peppers.

"I can't believe it," she said, fingering the stem of her glass of a 1988 Pommard.

"Can't believe what?" Richard said.

"That you do the kind of work you do."

"Oh, no," Spurge laughed, hoping to insure he could keep the subject floating rather than have it crash down all around them and blow up like a bomb.

"Don't worry," she said. "I could get used to going out like this."

He took her hand from across the table and put her fingers to his lips.

"I hope so," he said.

On Spring Street, she asked him to put her in a cab. When he protested, whimpering while pursing his lower lip and frowning, she said it was not that she would not sleep with him but that she would not sleep with him tonight.

* * *

"The future has already happened and we are moving towards it," Andrew said, passing the joint back to Max.

"We make the future and guide it towards us," Max contradicted him and then took a toke and held his breath.

"Oh, I don't know," Andrew said. "Does it matter?" He turned and looked at Harrison. The sky was dark and heavy. It was sure to snow.

"Have you heard from Miriam?"

"She does not answer my calls, and I'd just as soon not talk to her anymore."

"The children?"

"It's an expense I can bear."

"I mean not seeing them."

"They're ok. Richard's a nice man. He'll take good care of them, and with the monthly stipend I send plus the investments I've made for them, they'll each be able to go to college, and more."

"So now you are twenty-one again."

"Eighteen."

The Web was full of college students. Billie Holliday was on the juke box singing "It Was Just One of Those Things."

Derek was nervous. He was not comfortable standing in a bar hoping people would look at him and afraid, at the same time, that they would.

"You have not been doing this for long," Max said to him, touching his palm to the boy's cheek.

"No, sir," Derek said with a mid-western accent.

"Don't be nervous. You're very hot," Max said, pressing his palm against the young man's chest.

Derek blushed and dropped his eyes.

"Don't disappear," Max said, his palm dancing over the area of the boy's genitals.

"Say thank you," he said, as he cupped them in his palm.

"Thank you," Derek said, suppressing a giggle.

"Do you like him?" Max asked.

"He's very pretty," Andrew said. "I want to kiss him."

"I want to kiss him, too," Max said.

And he brought the boy to him and gave him a kiss full of his power. It made Derek shudder with desire. He wanted to be opened.

When Max let him go, Andrew did not wait but took his mouth with a delicate reach of his fingers and brought it to his and kissed him dreamily and long and languorously until the boy was helplessly dizzy with desire.

"Come," they said, leading him out of the bar.

"Who are you?" Harrison asked Derek once they were on the street and heading to his penthouse on Twenty-third Street.

"I was born in Kentucky. My father is a colonel in the army. My mother was a nurse but became a full-time housewife. We moved around, but we spent the last two years in Arizona. I'm studying theater at Columbia. Does that say enough?"

"Enough for now." Harrison smiled with a wink. "Theater!"

"My father doesn't like it. He wants me to go into the military."

Andrew took his other hand and kissed it gently, the upper side and then the open palm.

"But you know what you want," Max said.

The kid smiled grateful at the acknowledgement.

In bed, they stroked him and gazed at the opalescence of his flesh, and lost themselves in the voluptuous innocence of his fresh, spring-young body.

Andrew put his mouth to the boy's and felt swept towards him by the current of his breath. The ocean of his blood beat on the shore of his desire and with his kisses he swam inside Derek.

Derek held on to him and writhed, lost in the amplitude of his own sensations.

As he writhed like that, Harrison slid one hand beneath his jeans and slowly worked one finger into his granite ass. With the other hand he went under his t shirt and felt the warmth radiate from his chest. He took hold of one nipple between his thumb and first finger and slowly, gently began to knead it. His finger dug deeper into Derek; he increased the force with which he rubbed his nipples.

The boy saw the cloudless blue sky of Arizona rolling forever in translucent azure billows.

The End

Here is a sample from another story you may enjoy:

GIDEON ELLIOT

TABOO EROTICA

HYPNOTIZED

3 IN 1 BOXED SET

I'D KNOWN Jason since we were kids. I've always admired him – so much that it sometimes overwhelmed me. My admiration began with the way he looked. I always just enjoyed seeing him. He was a scrawny kid at the pool in the summertime, but lithe. He was adorable. When I think of him now, as I remember him during the summer, many years ago, when we were both seven, I can still see him as we undressed in the bungalow our families shared in Rockaway. He looked, stretching himself out of his little wet speedo, like nothing so much as a plucked chicken.

In his early teens he was smart and snappy and thoughtful, dressed sharp, got into gym and working out, as well as folk music – he taught himself guitar -- film noir, the Marquis de Sade, differential calculus, Nietzsche, and automobile engines. Girls talked about him, giggling with desire. He was easy around them, affectionate, cuddly, and, although he dated, he never got tied down to one girl friend. But none of the girls he dated expected him to, and none of them lacked for dates with other guys.

What was really beautiful is that he allowed me to love him. He was glad to accept it; he didn't push me away. When I looked at him with wondering eyes, with helpless admiration, he just grabbed me by the shoulder and horsed around for a minute.

Then he'd smile in the friendliest way. I didn't feel the least bit ashamed for showing my devotion. I'm always at ease with him but there are moments when I feel the excitement shaking inside me like I do with no one else. He's noticed it. And he doesn't hold it against me.

He'd go nuts if he couldn't accept love, 'cause he's a guy that everybody's crazy about, and he even can stay friends with girls who are dying for him but he won't sleep with them.

**

WE WERE in Butler library. We were seventeen. It was after ten, and the place was relatively empty. I'd managed to read all of Mill's *On Liberty* and I was thinking about the various possible extents and limits of human responsibility. I didn't get anyplace solid in my thought. I was spacey, floating, feeling like I was thinking but unable, the next moment, to remember exactly what I had been thinking.

Suddenly I heard fingers snap in front of my face and I saw Jason grinning. He'd just finished an assignment in differential calculus. If I had just had to squeeze my brain into that mold for two hours, I would not have been smiling.

"Where are you, Buddy?"

"I'm thinking about the limits of social responsibility and how you determine how much control any person can put on another; or an abstract group, like society, on the individual."

"Did anyone ever tell you that you lose yer bloom when you think."

"Cut the shit," I said, laughing at how beautifully he could move me from one place to another without even noticing it. "Aren't you tired of calculus already?" I said. "You're thinking all the time, and you haven't lost your bloom."

"Let's get some coffee," he said, throwing his arm round my shoulders.

"And stay up all night?"

"Don't worry."

Well, when Jason says "don't worry," you don't worry.

I couldn't get enough of him. I suppressed my sexual desire in order to be able to keep being with him. He didn't mind how I felt, but still I didn't want to make him uncomfortable by putting him in the awkward position of feeling like demands were being made on him, or of seeming like he was rejecting me. Most of the time it worked. I forgot about how much I wanted him and just enjoyed being with him the way we were. I forgot my sexual desire, or maybe it lingered as a ground bass giving greater resonance to whatever we did. I had become like an anorexic. Something else was more important to me than eating.

If you enjoyed this sample then look for **Hypnotized**.

Also by this Author

A Second Chance

The Recruiter

A Furtive and Hidden Embrace

Diamond Shadows

Displacement

Keen Obedience

Between Two Thieves

Heart's Desire

Sensual Surrender

Erotic Aggression

Don't Forget You Love Me

Unstable Emotion

The Hazard Game

A Knight in the Forest

Captured Emotions

The Mesmerist's Tale

On His Own

The Good Bitch

Succumb Touch

Blue Identity

About the Author

Gideon Elliot was born in 1981 in Wichita, Kansas.

He grew up in San Francisco and spends the greater part of the year, now, on one of the Cyclades Islands in Greece where he runs a jazz café, paints, writes poetry, and swims.

He has a small apartment in Greenwich Village, where he stays from the middle of November to the end of April and, during those months, manages an erotic men's clothing shop. He began writing erotic fiction at the age of fifteen.

You may also like the books by these authors:

DICK PARKER

The Horny

FARMHAND

HOT GAY ROMANCE EROTICA

Cory sat next to me and put his hand on my now hard cock.

"You must be happy to see me," he said.

"Damn right."

"I called a buddy of mine and he wants to meet you on Skype."

"Really? Who is it?"

"He's one of my friends from the modeling job."

"He's a porn actor too?"

Cory nodded.

I thought back to when we watched the video and I was getting excited about meeting this guy.

"Sure, let's do it," I said.

We went into the bedroom. Cory sat the computer up on the dresser and booted it up. He clicked on a couple of icons and soon a screen appeared and there was a really hot looking guy sitting at a desk.

"Hey, Tanner, how's it hanging?"

"Cory my man. It's long and loose and full of juice."

They talked shop about making another video soon. Then Cory had me move next to him and introduced me as Andy. I felt a little intimidated talking to another porn actor but the guy was real nice. He was dark skinned and had black hair and brown eyes. He was very good looking and from what I could see of him, he was very fit.

"Cory and I talked earlier, and he said you might be up for a little sex on cam," Tanner said to me.

"You mean with you watching?"

"Yeah, does that bother you?"

I looked at Cory and he shrugged.

"I thought you might like to try it with someone watching."

The idea made me hard as hell.

"I think I'd like to try that," I said.

Tanner smiled. Then he stood up in front of the cam and he was naked and his cock was standing up. He was a lot bigger than Cory or me.

"Wow," I said.

Tanner laughed and moved back from the cam so we could see him fully.

"Have you and he… you know," I asked Cory.

He nodded. Tanner sat back down at his computer.

"Well, let's see some fucking," he said.

Cory turned to me.

"We'll just do what we'd do if we were alone. Just forget the cam is watching us," he said.

I nodded. My cock was so hard it hurt. Cory stepped up to me and we began kissing. He wrapped his arms around me and ran them up and down my back. I put my face against his neck and sucked on it. Then I nibbled on his left nipple.

Meanwhile, Cory pulled my boxers down and squeezed my ass cheeks. My cock was leaking and all wet on the tip. Cory knelt down and took it in his mouth. I shuddered when he took it to the pubes.

"Oh, don't do that much or I'll cum," I said.

He let my cock slip from his mouth and stood up. He looked down at his cock and I pulled his boxers down and his boner popped up. I dropped to my knees and began sucking it.

"Nice," Tanner said.

I sucked Cory for a while and then we moved to the bed. Cory checked the cam and moved it a little. Then we lay on the bed making out.

"Can I fuck you?" he asked.

"Oh man, I was hoping you'd ask that," I said.

He had a condom in his hand and I had no idea where it had come from. He lay over on his back and I rolled it down his big cock. Then I lubed up my ass with spit.

"How do you want me?" I asked.

"On your back."

I lay down and pulled my legs up to my chest. He ran his finger up and down my ass crack.

"Nice butt hole," Tanner said.

"Watch this," Cory said. He knelt and began licking my asshole. It felt incredible. It felt amazing with his tongue pushing into my hole.

Then he moved up and I felt his cock pushing into me. I closed my eyes and the head slipped in. He stopped and let me get used to it.

"Okay?" he asked.

"It's a lot nicer this time," I said.

He worked his cock into me and began fucking me. I wrapped my legs around him and we made out as he rammed my ass. My cock was leaking like mad and so hard I could hardly stand it…

If you enjoyed this sample then look for The Horny Farmhand.

CHRIS JOHNS

Take it

OFF

HOT GAY ROMANCE EROTICA

The advert was quite specific.

Male pole dancers and strippers required for late night private members club. Don't apply if you have any inhibitions concerning nudity and displaying your wares.

Paul Hancock had just been made redundant and sat outside his apartment was a brand new BMW. Paul would do just about anything to keep it but without a job he wouldn't be able to meet payments. Despite having a good job for years, the only thing Paul owned was his flat. Everything else was the subject of hire purchase contracts, especially the Beamer.

The prospects of getting another well-paying job quickly were slim to non-existent. The best he could hope for was here in front of him. If he did this job he would be free during the day to job search. Although he wouldn't have said so himself, Paul was every gay man's wet dream and instant wet pussies on girls. His only problem was that he was shy and for this, the last thing he would have to be was shy, but where needs must.

With his heart in his mouth, Paul attended at the designated time and was surprised how many guys were there for auditions. They were led in to the main club and told to make themselves comfortable.

"The joint owners will see you one at a time but first will you fill in the form that is on all the tables. Also, take a Polaroid picture of yourself to attach to the form."

They made a game of taking the photos somehow eased the tension in the room.

"Now I don't want all you ladies getting excited when I pose for this picture", said one of the boys, as he slipped his shirt off one shoulder and got into a very provocative pose. They all laughed and fooled around in the photos.

When it was job done, the auditions started. The first one came out looking scared to death and told the others what was going to happen.

"I'm not staying. After you strip naked the girls start playing with you to get you hard, and they play with your arse as well."

He left, joined by several others. The five that were left looked at each other until one guy spoke.

"Huh, they won't get any joy from me. Women turn me right off."

Paul gulped and asked, "Are you gay then?"

The guy laughed and said, "Yeah, queer as a nine bob note," (no such thing of course).

He was the next one summoned and came out looking very pissed off.

"Bitches, they don't want me because I wouldn't get hard for them."

Four to go. One of the owners came through then looking less than happy.

"Something for you to think about. We'll do the rest of the auditions here. While we do them think about this. The club is a high end club for rich bitches like me, who want slutty action. You will be played with and you'll do two shows per night. The pay is £500 per night plus whatever tips you get, and they can be substantial."

One guy summed it up for the remainder.

"They can fuck me for that."

The owner smiled and came back.

"I'm pleased to hear that because they do like to see man on man sex culminating in someone getting a cock up their arse. The stripper that takes it usually gets tips that are more than his pay so give it some thought."

"Now, Paul, up on the stage, strip to the music that will start for you, use the pole and make it as raunchy as you can. If you get the job we'll supply special clothes and coaching to make it more erotic, but for now, do your best."

Paul was quite a good mover on a dance floor and started off with the music, no problem. He slowly undid his shirt and peeled it off throwing it at the audience of guys and the boss girls.

Using the pole he was able to toe off his shoes without having to bend, keeping the moves going. Trousers were next. He unclipped the top and slowly pulled down the zip. As they slid down his legs he grabbed the pole and swung round on it, kicking his trousers off as he did so. This next bit would test his resolve as he blushed almost scarlet. Now clad in just a pair of mini briefs and his socks one of the other guys, who was also gay, whistled and cat called and the boss girls clapped. Paul stopped then looking very embarrassed.

"You need to keep going if you want this job, pants off and a solid erection while you keep dancing and then you jump off the stage and start circulating being as erotic as you can for the clients."

Paul started dancing again and very slowly inched his briefs down until his arse was uncovered and the base of his cock, he was blushing like a school boy and feeling very nervous as he took about three or four minutes to slide them off completely. He swung round revealing his cute arse and then back again to show a very tasty cock. Getting redder by the second he started to play with himself until he had a solid erection. It looked impressive, about seven or eight inches uncut and standing out at 45 degrees to his tummy. He stood with his hands behind his head, feet astride and swaying to the music. When the music stopped he dropped to his knees and covered himself as best he could.

"The most important part starts now. The music will change and you'll jump down from the stage and wander among the tables. When one of the ladies touches you stay where you are until she loses interest and then move on. Depending what they do to you will usually determine the size of the note they stick in your waist string. The only men in the club will be one of the owners and you strippers, plus security at the door, but you won't see them. If one of the ladies indicates she wants to play with your arse, and even finger you, you will let it happen without hesitating, the same with any playing at the front, including make you suck one another."

Four very determined looking guys stayed. The other gay one eased the tension and made everyone laugh.

"Oh yes, me first, I can eat Paul's cock and let him feed it all to me in one push, Darling."

Paul blushed almost scarlet but he jumped down from the table and walked towards the lady boss making all the comments. She started caressing his cock and balls, watching his face.

"Open your legs wide, Paul."

If you enjoyed this sample then look for Take it Off.

HOT GAY ROMANCE EROTICA

Loving Rhett

AMY REDEK

It was, what, four years ago now that I thought that my world had collapsed. So let me tell you how that came about.

I had joined the Merchant Navy when I was fifteen and was almost constantly at sea for the next seven years before giving it up. It had been great visiting many foreign countries, but it was extremely boring when in the middle of one of the oceans. So I left and found work ashore in our local library.

At my interview at the council offices, it was the fact that I did an enormous amount of reading in those seven years, that I could name many authors and their books and so was given the job as assistant in that library.

Not blowing my own trumpet, I was six foot tall and quite good looking. Dark hair, clean shaven, clear blue eyes and a lovely smile. I got chatted up by quite a few women, seeing that I wasn't wearing a wedding ring, and very often had an evening out with quite a few. The one that attracted me the most was Caroline Traynor. I took her out many evenings, to the cinema, restaurants and walks in the park, in the summer time for the latter.

We'd been going out for over six months before I kissed her and was kissed back in return and another six months before I proposed to her. She agreed, and so six months later, we were married and moved into a rented flat.

It was a year later that she said that she wanted to have a baby, something that I wanted her to have, be it a boy or a girl didn't matter. We tried for nearly a whole year without success and eventually agreed to be checked out by a gynaecologist. After many tests, he said with a sorrowful look on his face that Caroline wouldn't ever be able to have a baby. He told us of the reasons why, which went over my head with not quite understanding exactly what was wrong. Caroline seemed to understand and cried as I held her as the nurse came into the office and asked for the doctor who had been talking to us, to see to a young woman who needed immediate attention.

For nearly an hour I held Caroline close to me, trying to comfort her as best as I could until the doctor came back into the room. He looked even worse that when he had told us of our problem as he sat down at his desk.

'The young lady I just went to see, had just died. It's heartbreaking when this happens. She knew she wasn't going to live and only had her baby for two days, so she asked me to find someone to take care of it. I remonstrated that her husband, who was there, that it was his child too, but he agreed with her that he wouldn't be able to look after a baby. I then told her of your problem and as sad as she was, she smiled and said that whoever it was, should be given her baby to love and cherish.

'She was failing rapidly and with the consent of her husband said I would try my best to see that the child had good parents to raise him. I was thinking of you then and stayed with her till she passed away and could leave her with her heart-broken husband to come and see if you would like to become the foster mother of this baby.'

I was flabbergasted at what he had said, but it really brightened up Caroline and asked if we could see the baby, which we could since it had been taken to the babies ward. So off we went and Caroline fell in love with the small baby that we saw and agreed there and then that she would love to be the mother of it.

The doctor was some kind of magician, for within a week in a court, we were given the baby to raise and see that he lived well. Caroline was over the moon and couldn't thank the doctor enough as we left the court to collect what would now be our baby and a week later, he was christened as Rhett. Coincidentally, my name is George Butler and she had loved the film "Gone with the Wind." Clark Gable played the part of Rhett Butler, so our adopted son was named after Gable's character.

If you enjoyed this sample then look for **Loving Rhett**.

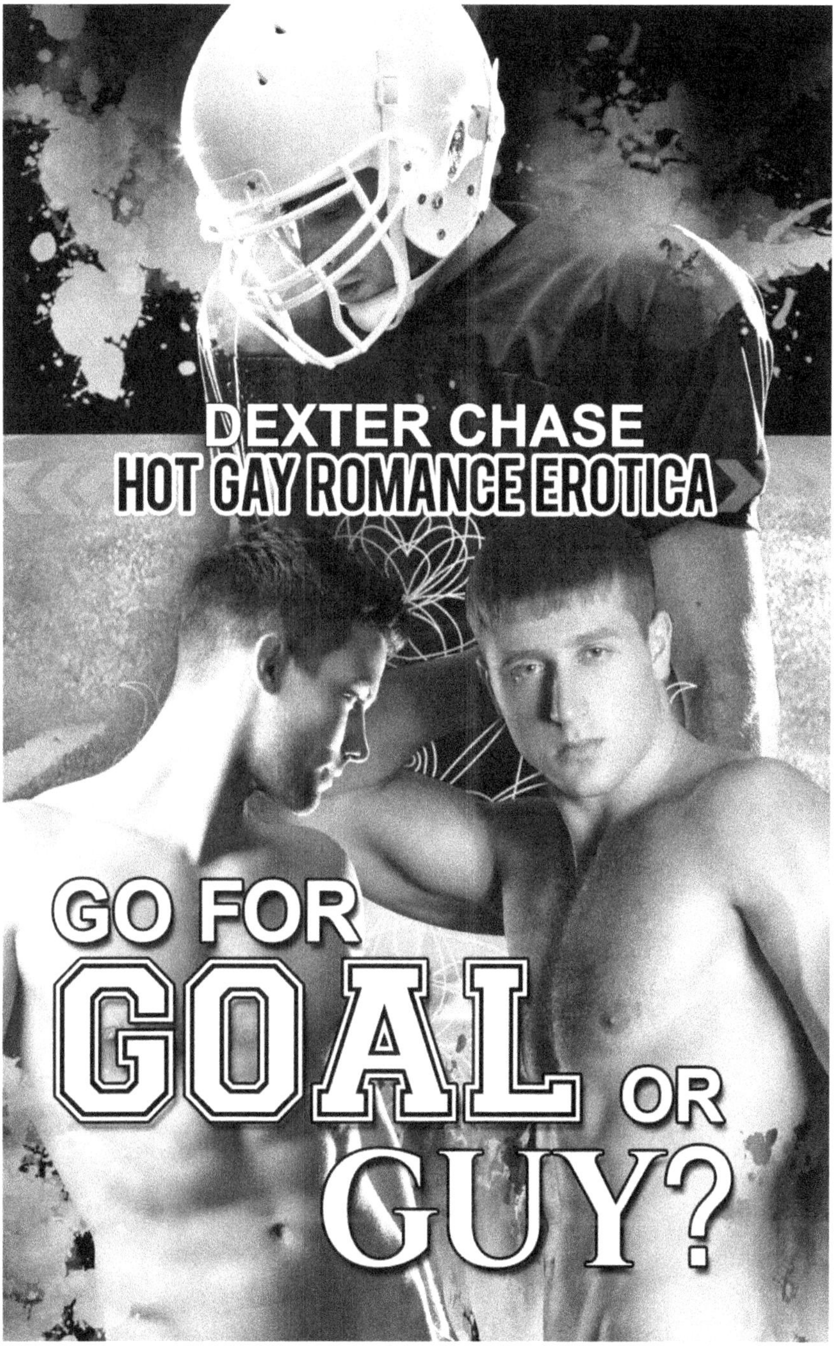
DEXTER CHASE
HOT GAY ROMANCE EROTICA
GO FOR GOAL OR GUY?

"Marcel, I'd like you to come with me to watch an academy game this afternoon"

That request was really the beginning for Luke Cross. He had been educated at a good private school, but Soccer was not played competitively so there were no inter-school matches for his talent to shine. In frustration he had played the occasional game for a local junior team. In his last season before graduating and sliding off to university Luke played for this team in a home match.

Tom Anders Jr. was a football freak and when his dad was home at a weekend, a rarity because Tom Sr. was a scout for Premier League team, Bedfont Rovers, he would drag him off to watch the local team play. On this Saturday, Tom sat mesmerized by the incredible skill of Luke Cross. The score was an embarrassing 16-0. Luke had scored 12 and assisted the other 4. It was a performance that had Tom's blood pulsing at an incredible rate. He collared the boy before he disappeared at the final whistle and made an appointment to call on him and his parents that evening.

"Luke, Mr. and Mrs. Cross, I won't beat about the bush. I think Luke is an amazing talent and I would like to sign him to the Academy at Bedfont. Unless I am very wrong he will be offered a seniors contract by the time he is 18."

The Cross family were blown away and once it was accepted that Luke would be tutored so that he sat his A Level exams on time a contract was signed.

"A car will come for you on Tuesday Luke. That will give you the chance to clear all your gear from your school and say your goodbyes."

When Tom had left, Luke's father sat down to talk with his son.

"What are you going to do about your sexuality, Son?"

"I'll have to keep it hidden Dad, at least until I'm an established player, maybe even forever. I'll do it if I can play soccer at the top level."

"Good boy, but now you understand why I wanted you to finish school. University can be put on hold and you can take up a place in years to come if necessary."

Luke gave his dad a hug and with tears in his eyes spoke to both parents.

"I was so lucky when parents were handed out. I got the best friends I could ever wish for."

Understanding was not an adequate word to describe the Cross's. Luke had talked to his dad about his sexuality when he was fourteen. He didn't understand the feelings he had about other boys. Sex education had talked about boy/girl sex, nothing about gay sex, and Luke hadn't been confident enough to bring up the subject. His father had given him enough detail for his curiosity to peak and he had explored on the internet. A year later he had his first gay experience when he and a friend had jacked off together, followed a while later by doing each other. Things hadn't progressed beyond that but Luke wanted to try blowjobs and anal. His father had accepted it when Luke had confirmed he was gay.

"I'm sorry, Dad, however much I try, thinking about girls doesn't do anything for me, but I spend half my life erect thinking about boys."

"I guess we don't have much choice deciding who we find sexy, Son. I think that is decided at birth. Just make sure you are careful, legal doesn't mean accepted."

That was how it was left and Luke became comfortable in his skin, knowing that he would have a difficult ride if his sexuality ever became known but also knowing he would always have the support of his parents.

The Tuesday morning was the start of a meteoric rise to prominence. Luke was coached at Bedfont Youth Academy for nearly six months until he had sat his A Levels and celebrated his 18th Birthday.

"Luke, Tom wants you to play in the reserves match this evening."

Tom had approached the manager of the senior squad and persuaded him to watch the reserve team match.

"Marcel, you can have my resignation if you think I have wasted your time at the end of the match."

That was good enough for Marcel Verona, Tom was the most successful scout he had ever worked with.

They watched the full 90 minutes with Marcel's mouth hanging open in shock at the performance of Luke Cross.

"I want him in my office first thing in the morning Tom. Has he got an agent yet?"

If you enjoyed this sample then look for <u>Go For Goal Or...Guy?</u>.

Wild
KNIGHTS
OF HEAT

Hot Gay Erotica

ANGUS MACGREGOR

"Hey, you think those boys are still awake?"

"You want more nut after all that?"

"I need to fuck a rookie tonight."

"Well, they are just down the hall. Tell them to get their asses in here."

Five minutes later, Sam's face was buried so deep in Ian's meaty ass it looked like his whole head was sliding inside. The rookie was on his belly, reaching behind to part his ass cheeks wide to let Sam have as much access as possible to his well-used hole. Sam pulled the boy's cock toward him so he could alternately suck the fat round head and Ian's smooth nutsack before drilling his hungry tongue deep into the young man's asshole yet again. The married man's face was wet with saliva as he feasted on the boy's hole, pulling it wide apart and probing the furry rosebud with his darting tongue.

While Sam dined on Ian's ass, Tom pushed Aaron's large, muscular legs apart and up toward his shoulders. The rookie's manhole was slippery with spit and Tom's fingers easily penetrated his muscle. His soft groans filled the dark room as two, three, then four fingers slid within the boy's pussy. Tom bathed his balls with his tongue, holding each one and sucking it gently at first, then harder until the rookie's belly quivered and he groaned anew. Aaron's penis leaked a steady flow of cock snot, a long string of silvery sweetness that dripped from the tiny lips of his throbbing cock, making a large sticky pool on his furry belly. Tom supped and sucked the rookie's hole and cock, feeling the tight virgin muscle give way until his four large fingers slid in and out with rapid ease. Aaron pulled around and took Tom's rigid pole into his mouth and swallowed it until his lips rested against the man's chrome ring. His eyes watered as Tom's cock stretched his mouth and filled his throat, his gag reflex coming in waves. Aaron looked over and saw Sam feeding Ian his thick penis, fucking his face with long deliberate strokes that buried his member deep into the rookie's mouth, flattening his nose into his thick nest of black pubes.

"Ok rook, breeding time," Sam hissed, pulling his cock out and slapping it noisily against Ian's soggy anus. The boy's eyes closed as the man's thick penis penetrated his hole and slid fully inside resting the man's gut and heavy sack against Ian's round ass. "Goddamn, I love plowing probie pussy," Sam said as began a rhythmic pumping into Ian's shitter.

"Oh my fucking God," Ian shouted as the pounding continued.

Tom pulled his cock out of Aaron's mouth, gripped the boy's thick, hairy ankles and let the tips of his penis rub against the spent asshole. Tom rocked back and forth twice and then pressed forward until the thick head of his cock split Aaron's sphincter. Tom's ass was a blur as he pounded again and again, deeply into Aaron's boyhole, ignoring the cries of pain. He finally leaned forward and pressed his mouth tightly against Aaron's, smothering out the shouts with deep kisses. Tom fucked the boy until he emptied his nuts again inside the ruined hole, white semen leaking from the stretched anus. Aaron's arms were tight around Tom's neck, the young man's kisses were deep and hungry. Across the bed, Sam shouted and ejaculated his thick load into Ian's spent asshole before collapsing on the sweaty rookie. Ian turned his head toward Sam and felt the man's tongue slide inside his open mouth.

"You are smokin' hot, buddy. I love fucking a rookie's ass like yours so much. Goddamn, you love getting pounded." With that, Sam slid down and began to lick and suck Ian's cum-filled hole while the rookie writhed and moaned.

"I'm gonna nutt," he gasped.

Sam flipped him over and gripped the young man's penis as it erupted blast after blast of thick semen into the married man's goateed mouth. When Aaron saw that, he felt his own orgasm explode and Tom lapped the hot sperm up from his hairy belly and leaking dick. The men lay still on the king-sized bed, soft sounds of kisses and breathing filled the warm bedroom. Aaron lay his head on Tom's big hairy chest and listened to the man's heart beat strong against his ear.

"I kind of love laying here like this," Aaron whispered, listening to Ian and Sam's soft kissing against his back. His ass was rubbing gently against his friend's. He reached over and let his hand slide down his butt to his legs and back up. Ian's hand found his and slid his fingers into Aaron's. Tom's large hand brushed against Aaron's face and kissed the rookie again, smiling at the sweaty face, tasting the mix of sperm and salt on his tongue.

"I kind of love it too, little buddy. Always have. You boys mean the world to me."

"You can fuck me any time you want, Tom," Aaron said.

Tom rested his nose against the rookie's nose. "You can count on it."

If you enjoyed this sample then look for <u>Wild Knights of Heat</u>.

www.ingramcontent.com/pod-product-compliance
Lightning Source LLC
Chambersburg PA
CBHW071347130626
46556CB00005B/2075